Bella Sara™

3

Jewel's Magic

HarperCollins ®, ®, and Harper Festival ®
are trademarks of HarperCollins Publishers.

Bella Sara: Jewel's Magic
Cover and interior illustrations by Jennifer L. Meyer.
Copyright © 2009 Hidden City Games, Inc. © 2005ñ2008 conceptcard. All rights reserved.
BELLA SARA is a trademark of conceptcard and is used by Hidden City Games under license.
Licensed by Granada Ventures Limited.
Printed in the United States of America.
For information address HarperCollins Childrenís Books,
a division of HarperCollins Publishers,
10 East 53rd Street, New York, NY 10022
www.harpercollinschildrens.com
www.bellasara.com

Library of Congress catalog card number is available.
ISBN 978-0-06-167334-4

❖

First Edition
09 10 11 12 13 CG/CW 10 9 8 7 6 5 4

Bella Sara™

3

Jewel's Magic

Written by Felicity Brown
Illustrated by Jennifer L. Meyer

HarperFestival®
A Division of HarperCollinsPublishers

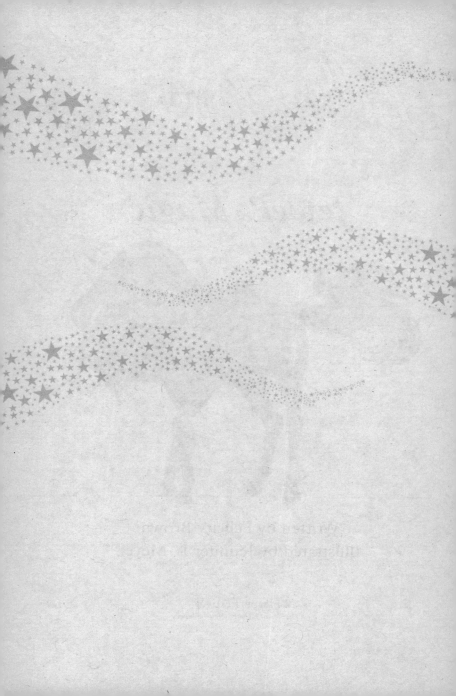

1

Shine Anders crinkled her nose and forked a lump of straw and manure from the stall floor. "Just because I love horses doesn't mean I should always have to muck stalls," she grumbled, throwing a shovelful into the wooden wagon resting in the center aisle of the Rolandsgaard Castle barn.

A laugh came from the neighboring stall, where a skinny stable boy groomed a big bay stallion. The boy peered over the stall divider. Wavy red hair fell across his eyes. He brushed it back impatiently.

"You're the one always whining that you don't get to spend enough time with the horses."

Shine smiled at her friend Jack. At thirteen, he was a couple of years older than her, but they got along well. "I guess you're right." She gazed at Bayler, the horse standing next to him. The stallion lifted his head to meet her eyes. Of all the horses, Bayler was her favorite. She couldn't go a day without visiting him, and he knew her well.

She smoothed back her dark ponytail. "Mrs. Marshall has given me kitchen chores all week long. When I saw the stables on my list, I guess I hoped that I'd actually be working with the horses." She smiled grimly at Jack.

Jack wiped the stallion's face with a soft cloth. "If you hurry and get finished, you'll have time to help me groom the last couple," he offered.

Shine picked through the straw, hefting a heavy section of wet straw into the wagon. She couldn't help but feel bitter. Life had become a hard business since she and her mother and grandmother had moved into the servants' quarters of the castle steward's grand house. It was humiliating to be employed as a servant at Trails End, living such a humble life right next to the splendor of Rolandsgaard Castle. Even though the castle had fallen into disrepair since Sigga Rolanddotter left, it still held magic in Shine's eyes. It was the grandest castle in North of North.

Shine let her mind wander, thinking about how different it all could have been. . . .

Bayler grunted. "He loves it when I rub behind his ears," Jack said.

"Tell him I'll give him an extra rubdown when I've finished the stalls," Shine said.

Bayler snorted, signaling that he'd heard. The soft black nose of the bay stallion was like velvet. His deep mahogany-brown coat was touched with black tips. Two weeks ago, Shine had walked into the town of Canter Hollow to see Bayler compete in the dressage ring. His moves were as graceful as those of any human dancer she'd ever seen. It made her heart flutter to watch him.

"When is your mother coming home?" Jack asked.

Shine kicked a clump of wet straw to the side, piling it before forking it. "She should have been back by now," she answered softly. "I'm worried. Grandmother won't admit it, but I know she is, too."

"Where was she was heading off to?"

Shine was silent. Should she share with Jack? He wasn't nasty like the Marshall children.

Still, she felt safer keeping it to herself. "Grandmother won't say," she replied, and there was no untruth in her answer.

Jack sniffed. "I know it's not my place, but I can't believe she left you alone with your grandmother so soon after your father. . . ." His voice trailed off.

In the silence that followed, Shine felt her emotions shift. She was annoyed with Jack for bringing it up, but only for a moment. The truth was, she had wondered the same thing. When Father was killed in the logging camp, it was almost more than she could bear. Moving in as the Marshalls' servants had added shame to pain.

Then Mother had decided she would try to find the Rolanddotter vault. It had been lost for so long that many believed its very existence was only talk, just a legend. But Shine's ancestors had been the official jewel crafters of Rolandsgaard Castle. The stories passed down were real. She just knew they were.

Still, she wondered if Mother would really be able to find the vault and bring home some of its fabulous treasures. And why couldn't she have taken Shine with her? *I could have helped*, Shine thought. *And I would love to see the Rolanddotter vault, full of all the treasures my ancestors made. . . .*

"Shine? Are you all right?"

Shine pushed her thoughts away. She shoveled the last of the manure from the stall and walked out, letting the door close heavily behind her. "I'm fine." Her voice was strong. She leaned the pitchfork against the wall and stepped into the stall with Jack and Bayler.

Bayler lowered his head, rubbing his nose against her cupped hand. Shine leaned into him, breathing in the warm, wonderful smell of horse. *This is heaven*, she thought, *pure heaven*. "Doesn't he remind you of Jewel?" she asked Jack.

"Hmmmm . . . they're both bay, but I don't know. I don't know the legendary horses the way you do," he answered.

"Father used to tell tales of them

around the fire at night." Shine sighed. Father had known everything about the horses and the legend of Sara, the child goddess of North of North. Sara had a special horse friend called Bella. Shine thought that if she had a special horse, it would be one like Bayler—or Jewel. "Did you know Jewel was carved from stone and came to life? She has sparkling gems set right in her forehead."

"I knew about the gems, of course," Jack said. "Everyone knows that. But I had never heard she was carved from stone. That's a nice story."

It's more than a story, Shine wanted to say, but she didn't. Not everyone in North of North believed the old legends were completely true. But Shine did.

"If you could pick one of the legendary horses as your own, who would you pick?" she asked Jack. "Jewel, Thunder, Nike, or Fiona?"

Jack grinned. "Easy question. I'd pick Fiona. She's born of fire—I like that idea." He laughed. "Besides, that's the one story I actually know."

"Well, I guess I have to finish the stalls," Shine said with a sigh. She picked up her fork and moved on to the next stall. Before long, she was done with the row. She pushed back her dark bangs and wiped sweat from her face. Then she remembered something that made her smile.

"Jack!" she yelled. "Grandmother is making apple pies today. I'm going to run to the kitchen to get some peelings for the horses." Bayler especially loved crunching the sweet, chewy apple skins out of Shine's palm.

Shine hurried along the path from the steward's stable to the big house. All the flowers were in bloom. The world had come alive with green in the last few months. Summer was upon them, and she loved everything about it. She inhaled deep, taking in the scent of flowers, grass, and hay. It was all tinged with the warm odor of wood smoke from the kitchen cookstove.

Grandmother's eyes lit up when she saw Shine. "Have you finished the stalls already?"

Shine nodded and watched her grandmother move unbaked pies to the stove top before leaning to pop them in the oven. Soft gray curls framed her face. Her apron was stained with cinnamon and streaked with butter. She looked just perfect to Shine.

"Yes, I finished, and now I have time to visit with the horses. Could I take the peels from your pies to feed them?"

Grandmother lifted her chin toward a bucket in the corner. "Take all you want," she said. "Don't be long though. I'll need your help with dinner."

Shine spotted her doll, called Gertrude, on the chair. "I'll take Gertrude, too," she said. "She likes visiting the horses."

Shine slipped Gertrude under her

arm, took the bucket by the handle, and headed out. Even though Gertrude had been without eyes for as long as Shine could remember, Shine always felt the doll was looking at her with a sweet expression. She wasn't a little girl anymore, but she still loved Gertrude. Gertrude was her only doll, one that had been passed down for generations.

Shine was barely out the door when she saw the Marshall children, Lucy and Jeremiah. She slipped from the path, hoping they wouldn't notice her, but it was too late.

"Where are you going, Shine? Don't you have chores to do?" Jeremiah asked with a sneer in his voice.

"What are you doing with that filthy doll?" Lucy chimed in.

"She's cleaner than you," Shine retorted.

Before Shine could dart away, Jeremiah was on her. He grabbed at the doll. Shine hung on, but Jeremiah was stronger. The doll slipped from her grasp.

Jeremiah threw Gertrude through the air to Lucy, who waited until Shine was almost upon her to toss the doll back to Jeremiah again.

The bucket of apple peels spilled where Shine had dropped it as she chased after Gertrude. "Stop it!" she yelled, clawing the air for Gertrude. Tears formed behind her lids. She would *not* cry. She hated them. "STOP!"

Jeremiah paused, the doll held in his hand like a missile. He stared at Shine. "Here," he said, flinging Gertrude into the dirt. "Take your dirty old doll. She's all you have, anyway, since your mother ran off and left you!"

Shine picked up Gertrude and glared at the pair. She was tired of them looking at her as if she were worthless. She'd meant to keep quiet about Mother, but she couldn't help herself. The words tumbled out.

"My mother did not leave me. She went to find the Rolanddotter vault, something *you* wouldn't know anything about!"

"The Rolanddotter vault?" Lucy giggled. "It's nothing but a fairy tale."

Shine raised her chin. "Laugh all you want," she said hotly. "For your information, it holds the Rolanddotter treasures. My mother has gone to bring some of them back. My family served as the Rolandsgaard Castle jewel crafters in the days of Sigga herself. We *made* half the jewelry that's in there! We have a right to the treasure of the vault."

Jeremiah roared with laughter. "A 'right'? You have no rights, you peasant!"

Shine hugged Gertrude close. "We're going to be rich, you'll see. Then you'll be the peasant!"

Jeremiah drew himself up angrily. He was a big boy, thick-bodied and tall. "You better watch how you talk. I'll get that doll from you while you sleep, and you'll never see her again. I'll burn her!" His eyes grew wide. "Poof! She'll go up in smoke!"

Shine couldn't listen. She spun away, scooping up the apple peels. Hugging Gertrude, she fled to the stable. The horses and Gertrude were the only two things that could make her feel better, and she needed them both right now.

Clink, clink, whoosh! Clink, clink, whoosh!
The sounds slid through the cobwebs of Shine's dreams. She shook away the sleep and sat up in her small bed. Summer winds whirled outside the window. A storm was brewing.

Clink, clink, whoosh! Clink, clink, whoosh!
There was that sound again. What *was* it? A shadow slid across the windowpane, a long hand with pointy fingers. No, it was just a tree branch tapping against the window. Shine sat still,

listening to the eerie sound. She leaned closer to the window. Every move she made caused the old wooden bed frame to creak.

A soft snore rose from the bed next to her. Grandmother slept soundly.

If only Mother were here, Shine thought. *Then I could sleep.*

When she closed her eyes Shine could picture her mother in her mind, her deep brown hair falling about her shoulders in thick layers, her face soft with love.

Shine opened her eyes, a hard lump in her throat. The shadows in the room enveloped her. She followed a thin shred of light coming in through the window. More shadows danced along the wall and settled in the corners. It was during these times late at night that Shine felt most alone. She stared into the gloom, shivered, and imagined monsters. She drew her knees to her chest. *It's only the dark,* she told herself.

She reached for a clay container of glow-food. She pinched a bit of plant pellet from the urn and sprinkled it into a globe-shaped lamp. Inside, glow-worms clicked their approval. As they began to eat, a greenish glow spilled from the lamp. It was faint at first, and then brighter as more worms awoke to eat. The light and the tiny sound of the worms chewing comforted Shine.

She stretched out, pulling the sheet up to her nose. When she was young, her mother had told her how her great-grandmother—and *her* mother and grandmother before her—had worked as official Rolandsgaard Castle jewel crafters. Shine was sure that the stories had changed over years of telling, but she loved hearing them just the same.

Gertrude had come into the family back then. One of Shine's great-great-something-grandmothers had been given the doll—by whom, Shine didn't know. That story was lost in the past.

Shine reached out to pull Gertrude close, but the doll was not on the pillow.

Frowning, Shine felt under the sheet, her hands sliding back and forth, all the way to the bottom of the bed. Her hands scrabbled among the covers, feeling for the soft cloth body and twisted red yarn hair. Where was Gertrude?

She felt under her pillow. No doll there.

She fell to her knees on the floor, sweeping her arms under the bed.

Where was Gertrude?

Shine kneeled by the side of the bed, her head bowed, her heart beating wildly, staring at her empty hands. She knew where Gertrude was. She had no doubt.

Jeremiah had kept his promise.

2

$\mathscr{S}$hine lay awake in the dark for
what felt like hours, kneading the
covers between her fingers. *Jeremiah stole
Gertrude! Jeremiah stole Gertrude!* The
chant kept running through her thoughts.
She was so upset that she couldn't even
focus on what to do about it.

She must have fallen asleep at
last, because the next thing she knew,
Grandmother was calling her name to
wake her up.

"Shine?" Grandmother leaned
over the bed, brushing Shine's dark hair

from her face.

Shine shot into a sitting position. "Gertrude!" she exclaimed. She looked into Grandmother's gray eyes. "Gertrude is gone," she said, her voice breaking.

Grandmother sat down on the bed, looking puzzled. "What are you talking about, child?"

The pain had rushed back, filling Shine. "Yesterday, Jeremiah said he was going to take Gertrude and burn her," she told Grandmother. "And then last night I woke up—and I couldn't find her. He must have come into our room while we slept." She squeezed her eyes shut, willing herself not to cry.

Grandmother patted Shine's leg. "Are you sure you had her with you when you fell asleep?"

"I never go to bed without Gertrude."

Grandmother stood. "My darling girl, stop fretting. I promise we'll find her," she said. "But right now we have to start breakfast for the Marshalls."

Scowling, Shine climbed out of bed. She pulled a frock from the wooden chest that held her few belongings. "I hate fixing breakfast for them," she said. "I despise them!"

Grandmother sighed and stroked Shine's hair. "I tell you what. Why don't you take the morning off? Breakfast is an easy meal. I can do it alone."

"But, Grandmother—"

"Oh, pooh. Don't you think I can handle a few flapjacks?" Grandmother wrapped her arms around Shine, hugging her tight. "You're still a child. Children need time to play every now and then.

"Come," she went on, motioning Shine to follow her across the small room. She opened up a wooden chest, kneeled down, and rooted through a small stack of clothing and blankets. "I have something in here that will get your mind off your troubles," she said.

Grandmother laid a folded square

of white cotton cloth on the bed. She unfolded it carefully. Inside was a small collection of stone and pottery beads.

Shine sat on the bed, fingering the cloth, studying the beads. She felt a tinge of bitterness. *Why couldn't they be real jewels?* she thought. After all, she was a jewel crafter by blood.

The aqua-colored stone beads were marbled with tan lines. There were also a rounded piece of granite and an assortment of colored clay beads. Someone had bored a hole in each. Also inside were a small roll of wire and a pair of nippers, the handles worn from years of use.

They were very pretty, Shine had to admit. The aqua would contrast beautifully with Bayler's black mane, if she made him a forelock ornament. In spite of her frustration, she felt a twinge of excitement.

"Thank you, Grandmother." She squeezed Grandmother's hand. "You're so good to me."

Alone in the room, she set to work, stringing the beads in a pattern. She joined two wires together to make the piece double stranded.

But as she worked, the thought of what Jeremiah had done kept intruding. *I'll catch him alone,* she thought. *I'll get Gertrude back—and I'll make him pay for taking her.*

The trouble was, Jeremiah was nowhere to be found all day. His mother had taken him and Lucy to visit friends in Canter Hollow, and they were not due back until after supper.

To make matters worse, Shine was unable to get into Jeremiah's room to search for Gertrude. The steward, Mr. Marshall, was having the house worked on. The entire second story was blocked off by carpenters and stonemasons for most of the day.

Shine grew increasingly worried as the hours went by. She was reasonably sure Jeremiah hadn't carried out his threat and burned Gertrude last night. But what if he was going to do it today? What if he and his snooty friends in Canter Hollow were standing around a roaring fire right now, laughing as they watched the doll crackle in the flames? She had a hard time believing even Jeremiah could be that cruel—but there was no way to be sure.

By day's end, Shine was exhausted. She'd spent most of the afternoon fetching water for the stonemasons and running errands for the head carpenter. She was reluctant to go to bed without having confronted Jeremiah, but there had been no chance. "It'll keep until tomorrow," Grandmother told her with a hint of exasperation. "You must stop fretting, Shine."

Now it was night again, and Shine was awake—again. The moon was full. It shone through the tiny window and cast a swath of white light across wide wooden floorboards. Grandmother's snores usually lulled Shine to sleep, but tonight was different. Tonight her arms were empty.

What would happen if she slipped into Jeremiah's room and searched for Gertrude? If she crept into the main wing, she would be discovered for sure. The Marshalls would definitely be angry. Shine didn't want them to take out their anger on Grandmother.

Finally, Shine climbed out of bed. It was no use trying to sleep when her thoughts were at such a boil. She wandered outside to watch the Auroborus. Something about the way the lights danced magically in the night sky above Trails End brought her a sense of peace— something she desperately needed.

Shine walked slowly, following the Winding Byway. Her nightgown flapped against her legs as she followed the path of moonlight. The breeze lifted strands of her dark hair to float about her face. She brushed them away and kept walking.

In the distance, a bird's sad song drifted through the hollow. *Chee-caw. Chee-caw.* Across the way, there was an answering call. *Chee-caw. Chee-caw.* A fine layer of goose bumps rose across Shine's shoulders. The path she was on turned, angling down the hill.

She could see lights shimmering on the ridge across the way. She knew they came from the great world tree, Drasilmare. A few lights still glowed from inside the homes that hung like birdhouses from the tree's huge branches. Then, one by one, they began to go out. *Everyone is sleeping,* Shine thought. *Everyone but me.*

She gazed over the valley. The moon lit the hillside, turning bushes and trees silver. It slid across the water and onto the next hill. It made everything look magical.

Shine kept walking, following the shoreline of Teardrop Lake. The lake was large, wrapped with silvery-green trees and bushes of all varieties. Shine knew its water flowed from the crying statue of the goddess Sara. It was told that Sara, heartbroken over the loss of her parents, sat in this spot year after year, weeping. Her tears pooled, becoming a puddle, then a stream, and then the lake.

Leaves rustled. Shine followed the breeze, gazing across at the Sacred Memories Garden and the statue of Sara. *She lost both her parents, like me*, Shine thought. The fear she'd been pushing away—the fear that Mother might never return—rose up and threatened to swallow her. First, she'd lost Father, then Mother. She'd managed to keep the sadness away until now—but somehow, the loss of Gertrude was the last straw. It made everything else unbearable.

Shine kneeled by the lake's edge. Tears welled up until they overflowed and ran down her cheeks. A single teardrop slid into the pool of water at her feet. It began to shimmer. Another teardrop struck the lake's surface. Where it hit, the water surged with life.

Shine straightened up. Wiping away her tears, she watched lights begin to dance on the water. Her pulse quickened. She felt as if something big was about to happen.

She sat very still. On the rippling surface, a shimmery horse appeared. The horse at first looked fragile, thin, and iridescent, but then color began to fill in. A beautiful mahogany bay mare took shape. When she shook her head, a spray of glistening water was cast aside. It sparkled like fireworks in the moonlight, and the horse stepped forth.

The mare reminded Shine of Bayler, dark and glistening. She took another step and lowered her head to Shine. A sparkling array of jewels covered her forehead and ran down her nose.

Shine's mouth dropped. It was Jewel! The real Jewel! The horse she had loved in her father's tales was alive—and standing before her.

3

Jewel lowered her head to Shine. Her velvety nose caressed the girl's cheek. Shine reached out to stroke the mare's soft muzzle.

Jewel did not back away. She moved forward, gazing at Shine with an intensity that took her breath away.

"Hello, Jewel," Shine said. Her heart was beating fast, her mind trying to grasp that this was really happening. The mare rubbed her head against her. Shine's eyes were drawn to the gems. They glistened and sparkled, an array of lights and colors. "You're as beautiful as I imagined."

All around them, the garden began to twinkle. The air seemed charged with electricity. *Something important is about to happen here,* Shine thought, *just like something important happened here all those years ago, when Jewel was a filly.* She moved to stand beside the mare. She stroked the soft brown neck, raking her fingers nervously through the ebony mane.

To Shine's amazement, a scene began to play out before them. Shimmering, ghostlike figures hung in the air just above the grass.

Even though Jewel was right beside her, Shine also saw the mare in the scene with four other horses, all yearlings. Shine recognized them as Fiona, Thunder, and Nike, the other legendary horses. They gazed at the entrance to the garden. Shine followed their gaze and saw a girl of about twelve, side by side with a glorious white horse. The girl lifted her hand, and a butterfly landed briefly in her palm. Then it lifted off into the air, fluttering over the white horse. The girl stepped forward and kneeled to read the memorial stone. Her face was full of sadness.

That's Sara! Shine realized with a shock. She was witnessing a scene from the ancient past, when Sara first came to visit the memorial to her parents.

If the girl is Sara, the white horse can only be Bella, Shine guessed. She thought of the stories she'd heard all her life. *They're not just stories! It's all real,* she thought.

She watched as Sara sat back on her heels. A pair of playful lotus hedgehogs approached Sara, and she reached out to run a hand over their coarse fur. Then she plucked a lotus flower and set it upon the lake. The flower floated lazily, following the current past a family of bubble turtles. Their heads bobbed

above the water.

Sara hugged Bella close. "Something terrible has happened," she murmured to the horse. Although her voice was soft, Shine could hear it clearly, almost as if Sara were speaking into her ear instead of Bella's. "Sigga Rolanddotter and all her descendants have been banished! The safekeeping of all the horses in North of North has fallen on my shoulders." Tears rolled down Sara's cheeks.

Bella nuzzled Sara's hand and blew out a soft breath. Sara paused with her head cocked as if she were listening to something. "I hope so, too, Bella," she said after a moment. "When she chose the love of a mortal man, Sigga broke the rules that Álfather laid down for the Valkyries. But her crime was to follow her heart. I hope someday she will be forgiven for that. She may never return to North of North, but perhaps her children's children will."

Jewel stamped a hoof gently. Shine shifted her weight to lean against the mare, and Sara began to speak again.

"The Rolanddotter vault has been hidden, protected by secrets and spells. It will keep the Rolanddotter treasures safe from looters and treasure seekers until someone from Sigga's house returns to North of North," she told Bella. "All the Rolanddotter jewels are locked inside. Sigga has given me the key." She pulled something from inside her robe.

Shine saw a flash of red yarn hair and a small black-shod foot. She let out her breath in a whoosh. It was Gertrude! Sara was holding Gertrude in her hand!

"I'm confused," Shine said aloud.

Sara took no notice. "I will give the doll to Jewel," she said. Bella nick-ered.

"You agree?" Sara asked the great horse. "It is best that Jewel keep the key safe."

Shine spun around to face Jewel.

"Wait. *Gertrude* is the key to the Roland-dotter vault?"

Jewel gazed into Shine's eyes.

For now, Shine put aside her confusion about how a doll could be the key to a vault. There were too many other questions buzzing through her mind. "And you've been watching over her all this time?" *And over me?* she added, but only in her thoughts.

Jewel's head bobbed up and down in a definite nod.

Shine looked back at the garden, but the scene had fizzled out. Sara and Bella were gone. The leaves moved gently on the soft summer breeze.

Shine's thoughts whirled. *But Gertrude is gone.* She turned back to Jewel. "Did you come to help me rescue Gertrude from Jeremiah?"

Jewel nodded again. Then the mare lowered her head and went down on a knee, bowing.

"What? Oh—" Shine caught her

breath. "You want me to get on your back?" Feeling daring, she grasped a handful of ebony mane, slipped a leg over the mare's back, and climbed aboard.

Jewel pawed the ground impatiently, and then raised her head and whinnied. Shine felt the mare's body tremble beneath her.

"You're right," she said. "Let's get going."

Wind brushed Shine's cheeks. Her dark hair blew back and the ground rushed past below as Jewel trotted toward the castle.

Hold on, Gertrude, Shine thought. *We're coming to save you!*

4

hine leaned over Jewel's neck, gripping the mare's sides with her knees tightly. Jewel responded by breaking into a full gallop. Down the hill they flew. Wind burned Shine's eyes.

The castle and the steward's home were just ahead, rushing to meet them. Jewel slowed and slipped into an extended trot. Shine rocked gently as the mare nosed open the broad doors of the steward's house.

Jewel's hooves clip-clopped rhythmically. Shine couldn't believe she was riding right into the Marshalls' house on the back of such a glorious mare! She felt as tall as Drasilmare, strong and proud. She wanted to pinch herself, to make sure she wasn't dreaming.

Jewel shot up the stairs, taking them in great leaps. Shine laughed out loud when she realized Jewel knew her way around. She really *had* been keeping an eye on Gertrude! When Jewel soared, Shine's heart soared, too. With Jewel, anything was possible!

Down the hall the great mare pounded, sliding to a stop in front of Jeremiah's bedroom door. Then she stood, head lowered, waiting for Shine to take charge.

Shine's heart thudded. She reached down to pat Jewel's neck. Power, strength, and a newfound confidence shot through her like lightning. She leaned down, grasped the wooden doorknob, and pushed the door open. She sat tall when Jewel stepped into the bedroom.

Shine had never been inside Jeremiah's room before. It was large, with windows that looked out on the wide lawn below. Jeremiah lay in his bed, blankets up to his chin. Moonlight streamed in through the windowpane and cascaded across his face. He looked angelic, but Shine knew better.

Amazingly, he didn't stir as Shine and Jewel approached the bed. Shine wondered if some of the same magic that had shown her the vision by Teardrop Lake was now keeping Jeremiah asleep. Well, whether it was magic or just plain luck, she was not going to question it.

She slipped from the mare's back and kneeled to look under the bed. The wooden floor was barren of all but a few dust balls. There was no sign of Gertrude.

What if he really had burned her, like he said he would? Shine felt her anger rising again. How could Jeremiah get away with such awful behavior? Why was life so unfair?

She saw an overstuffed armchair in the far corner of the room and slid forward on her knees, looking behind the chair. Maybe Gertrude was hidden there.

The space behind the chair was empty. But just as she was about to turn away, Shine saw a tiny foot wearing a black cloth shoe, sticking out from under the chair's dust ruffle. She knew that shoe!

Shine pulled Gertrude out from under the chair. The doll was draped with cobwebs but appeared otherwise unharmed. Not burned! With a sudden lump in her throat, Shine stroked Gertrude's red hair and touched her face. "I found you," she whispered.

Jewel pawed the floor. The sound of the solid hoof scraping the wide wooden floorboard finally woke Jeremiah. He sat up, rubbed his eyes, and stared at the strikingly beautiful horse that stood in the middle of his bedroom.

His eyes were wide and fearful, and he wrapped his arms around his knees. Then he saw Shine with Gertrude in her arms.

"You!" he exclaimed.

Shine stepped next to Jewel. She leaned against the mare, feeling another spike of courage. "Yes, me. Gertrude is mine. You had no right to take her, and you will never touch her again!"

Jeremiah looked momentarily stunned. Then he opened his mouth to yell for his mother.

Jewel pawed the floor again. Jeremiah froze with his mouth open. The gems in Jewel's forehead were alight, a dancing light show of color. Dazzled, he closed his mouth slowly.

Shine grasped a handful of black mane and vaulted onto her new-found friend's back. She guided Jewel out the door, leaving Jeremiah staring after them, completely awestruck. They walked down the hall quietly, and then down the steps.

Outside, on the lawn, Shine slipped from Jewel's back, feeling exuberant. Jewel nuzzled her arm, and she wrapped her arms around the mare's strong neck. "I did it!" she exclaimed. "*We* did it!"

Jewel nickered, her breath tickling Shine's arm.

"Jewel. . . ." Shine's voice faltered for a moment as nervousness overcame her. She had an idea—an incredible idea—but she wasn't sure if Jewel would think it was wise.

But then confidence bubbled back up. Riding a horse into Jeremiah's room in the middle of the night to find a stolen doll was not something that most people would call "wise," and yet Jewel had done it with her. They had done it not because it was wise, but because it was right!

"Jewel," she said again. "My mother left to find the treasure vault of Sigga Rolanddotter. She hasn't come back. I don't know what—" She broke off, swallowing down the fear that something terrible had happened to her mother. *No! Mother was all right!*

"I'm sure she is still looking," Shine went on in a stronger voice. "Only, you see, she doesn't know how to find it. But you do."

Jewel took a step backward and shook her head so that her mane swung side to side.

"Well, you must have *some* sort of idea. And we also have the key." Shine held Gertrude up. "So I was thinking, will you help me find the vault?"

Jewel was staring at her, and it struck Shine suddenly that Jewel might not *want* her to find the vault. It was Jewel's job to protect it.

"Please!" she said. The words came out in a rush. "If we look for the vault, we might find Mother, too, and I can bring her home. And besides, my ancestors are the Rolandsgaard Castle jewel crafters. And Gertrude has been in my family for years and years, and she's the key. I believe . . ." She took a deep breath. "I believe I'm *meant* to find the Rolanddotter vault!"

Jewel lowered her head thoughtfully. Then she nodded and stepped forward, pushing her nose into Shine's chest.

Shine giggled and rubbed the mare's head. "Itchy spot, huh?" she asked. Her heart was dancing. Jewel would help her! Together they would find the Rolanddotter vault, and Mother, and the Rolanddotter treasure, and then they'd be rich, and everything would be perfect!

And Jeremiah will be sorry, too, a little voice inside her whispered.

Shine turned toward the kitchen. She'd need some food to take along. Thinking of the kitchen made her remember—Grandmother! Shine needed to let Grandmother know where she was going and why. But she didn't want to wake Grandmother up and run the risk of being told she couldn't go.

First things first. In the kitchen, Shine opened a cabinet and pulled out a loaf of crusty bread. Taking a knife from the top of a buffet, she cut three slices from a round brown loaf, wrapped them in a square of cloth, and tied it tight. She opened the pantry door, grabbed four apples from a bushel basket, and shoved everything into a cloth sack that she tied to her belt. The last thing she took before leaving the kitchen was an empty lantern from the shelf.

Next, Shine led Jewel into Mrs. Marshall's parlor. She found a quill and a well of ink on Mrs. Marshall's desk. She pulled out a roll of parchment, smoothed it open, and hoped Mrs. Marshall would not notice it was gone. She dipped the pen in the ink and began to write.

Dear Grandmother,

Please don't worry when you find that I have gone. I can't tell you everything,

*but tonight I met a beautiful bay mare . . .
Jewel! She is going to help me find Mother,
and maybe even the vault! Know that I
am safe with Jewel.*

Shine paused, dipped her pen in the ink, and continued.

*If the Marshalls ask about me, tell
them I ran away.*

Shine smiled. She wondered what Jeremiah would say to that.

Jewel stood quietly watching her write, her broad forehead beside Shine's face, the delicate muzzle hanging over the girl's shoulder, almost touching an arm. Shine looked up. Jewel was patient, kind, and full of love. How could she convey that to Grandmother? How could she convince Grandmother that she would be safe?

*Jewel will take care of me. I love you,
Grandmother.*

She dipped the pen in the inkwell a final time and signed her name.

Shine

Jewel followed Shine up the stairs again to the room she shared with Grandmother. She crossed the darkened room. Feeling around for the lamp, she opened the top and reached inside. She scooped up three glowworms and slipped them into the lantern. Next, Shine put on the dress she had worn that day. She threw a jacket on over it. The night was warm, but it might not stay that way . . . and besides, she didn't really know how long she'd be gone. She tucked a handful of glow-food pellets into her pocket.

At last, Shine stepped close to the bed and looked down at her grandmother. Grandmother's eyes were closed, her gray curls tousled about her head. Shine listened to the soft snores she had come to love. Shine's eyes were unexpectedly wet as she laid the letter on the pillow and turned to go.

Then Shine and Jewel walked down the steps together, out the front door, and into the night.

5

"Do you know where we start?" Shine asked Jewel. A thread of worry had begun to wind its way through her mind.

Jewel nodded briskly. The gemstones on her forehead glowed. The mare's hooves click-clacked on the stone walkway.

From the inside pocket of Shine's jacket, where Shine had tucked her for safekeeping, Gertrude's face peeked up. Shine smiled down at her beloved doll. "If only my mother had known that

Gertrude is the key," she said to Jewel. "Mother went looking for treasure, never knowing she left the key at home."

Jewel made her way around the outside of Rolandsgaard Castle. She stopped at the back of the palace, in front of the stone wall.

Shine recognized the spot. She'd played here with Gertrude when she was younger. The soft, grassy area always felt secluded and safe. "Why are we stopping here?" she asked.

Inside her head, Shine saw an image of Jewel rising on her hind legs before the wall. She gasped. Jewel was trying to tell her what was about to happen.

Quickly, she made sure Gertrude was secure and grabbed a handful of thick black mane, hanging on tight to the mare with clenched leg muscles. "Ready," she said.

Still, it took everything she had to stay aboard when Jewel rose on her hind legs. The mare's forehooves danced

in midair. She came down hard, strong black hooves striking the stone wall. The massive blocks swung wide, opening up to a tunnel.

Shine stared into the passageway, her heart pounding. Cool air wafted out, mixing with the warm night breeze. "Is this the way to the vault?" she asked.

Jewel's answer was in her step. They entered the tunnel.

Within a few steps, the temperature dropped drastically. Shine shivered. The opening slammed shut behind them, taking even Jewel by surprise. She spooked, jumping forward in a single leap. Shine held on until the mare stopped and stood braced, her legs spread wide. Shine patted the sweaty neck. "It's all right," she said. "We're not hurt."

Jewel nickered. The sound echoed down the tunnel and back again.

Shine rubbed at the goose bumps on her arms. Reaching down, she closed her fingers around Gertrude. "Whatever happens, we are in this together," she said, speaking not only to Jewel, but to Gertrude, too.

There was just enough light to see the outline of the tunnel. Shine took a deep breath. A dank smell, like root cellars and rotting forest leaves, filled her nostrils. The passage before them wound down, down, down under the ground. She touched the lantern tied to her apron, and then felt in her pocket for the glow pellets. They were there. Reassured, she sat up a bit straighter.

Jewel's hooves made a solid *thunk, thunk, thunk* sound on the dirt floor of the tunnel. Down they went, through the twisty passageway. Shine's eyes adjusted quickly to the dimness. There were no glowworms on the walls, but some of the rocks seemed to emit a faint, eerie radiance. Rock outcroppings loomed out from the blackness from time to time. Shine saw a group of warbled snufflebats hanging under a ledge. The presence of life was comforting, even if they were only bats.

After a while, the narrow tunnel spilled out into a wider, grander tunnel with a river running down one side. In the distance Shine could see a horseshoe-shaped arch. "The Treasurebow," she said aloud, recognizing the arch from more old stories. "We're in Stonelory, aren't we, Jewel?"

Jewel whinnied.

Stonelory! This ancient sea cave had once been a mine. Father had spoken of it. Some of the most incredible gems in the Rolanddotter collection had come from Stonelory. Now, the waterway gave passage to those traveling into the royal water stables. But the vast web of mining tunnels lay unused and unexplored.

Shine and Jewel traveled on the path next to the luminous turquoise waterway. A great silver fish leaped from the water, flipped in the air, and then sluiced through the water again. "Look at that!" Shine exclaimed. Her eyes sparkled, taking in the soft green-shaded mosses that grew on the edge of the water and listening to the pleasing sounds of hoofbeats on stone and gurgling water. It was beautiful here! Not dead at all!

With such beauty around her, it was hard not to relax. Besides, Shine had faith that, with Jewel's help, she would find the Rolanddotter vault. And then her life would change forever.

Shine touched Gertrude's head. "We'll find the vault and show those bratty Marshalls," she said to the doll. "We'll be rich. And Mother will never need to leave me again. Won't she be amazed when I open the vault? Won't *everyone* be amazed?"

Jewel's ears swiveled back as she listened to Shine's chatter. She was quiet, though, and Shine had the uncomfortable feeling the mare didn't entirely approve of what she was saying. She fell silent.

They followed the water for a while. Then they took a turn away from the wide, brightly lit tunnel, into one that had less room for maneuvering. They turned to the right, then to the left, then to the right again, then left, then right, all the while moving deeper underground. Just when Shine thought they must surely end up in some other world, the tunnel spilled out into a large arena.

It was a colossal riding ring. Shine's face broke into a smile. "I wonder if this was one of Sigga's training arenas," she said.

Jewel's head came up excitedly. She pranced sideways. Shine glanced around the room. There were no exits, no other tunnels except the one they'd come through. It seemed this was the end of the line.

If this riding ring is the tunnel's end, where's the vault? she asked herself.

Did we go the wrong way?

Puzzled, she glanced again at the riding ring. Its level floor was coated in springy wood chips, its fence rails painted a gleaming white. The rocks in the ceiling glowed softly, lighting the whole cavern with a warm radiance.

Dressage, Shine thought. *This ring is perfect for dressage.*

Jewel seemed to react to Shine's thought. She began to prance, pumping her legs higher and higher, dancing in fluid motion.

Shine remembered watching Bayler compete in the event in Canter Hollow. She'd paid attention to every detail that day. Now, she sat up straighter and dropped her legs lower, imagining a saddle and trying to sit as the rider had on Bayler. A spotlight above the arena snapped on, spilling a cone of light onto the floor of the ring.

Jewel circled the arena. The air swept against Shine's face. Jewel stretched out, breaking into an extended trot and then a canter. Shine felt like she was floating. In the center of the ring, Jewel stopped, trotting in place, retaining an even rhythm with incredible bouncy movement. There was a brief moment of suspension between her footfalls.

Shine's mouth fell open slightly. The move Jewel was doing was the piaffe, just the way Shine had seen it performed by a golden palomino at the event in Canter Hollow! Even in her wildest dreams, Shine had never imagined sitting astride a horse like Jewel, performing the most intricate of dressage maneuvers. *If only Lucy and Jeremiah could see me now,* she thought. *They'd be so jealous!*

Above them, the light grew brighter, filling the room. Delicate tendrils of mist swirled in the beam. Jewel performed a capriole, kicking her back legs out, curling her front legs beneath her and rising into the air, floating for brief seconds as if suspended by wires.

Glowing dust began to rain like pollen, glittering gold. The arena grew even brighter.

A large light source swirled downward, slower and slower, closer with each swirl. In awe, Shine watched it. Closer and closer it came, until she realized what it was . . . a glowing orchid, made of light.

Jewel moved closer. Shine stared at the lustrous white flower. *I want to pick it. But how do you pick light?* What a silly idea! Still, the urge was strong. Tentatively, she reached out and grasped the flower's stem in her hand.

Energy surged through her. She gasped and let go of the flower, rubbing her tingling arm and hand. Then she gasped again, this time in wonder, as a picture appeared on the wall beyond. It was a map of sorts. It showed tunnels twisting and turning and intersecting. At every intersection, the turn to the left glowed.

"It's telling us the way! We have to remember to always turn left!" Shine exclaimed.

With a grating sound, a large boulder in the far wall sank into the ground, revealing a tunnel behind it.

Jewel whinnied. Shine squeezed her legs to move the mare forward. "Come on, Jewel. Let's follow the map."

Shine twined strands of soft black mane around her fingers as Jewel stepped through the tunnel's opening. *No wonder others haven't found the vault,* Shine thought. *It took a horse that knew dressage to reveal the way!*

6

The new tunnel was just as twisty as the one before, but a lot darker and mustier. Shine was getting tired. She stretched and tried to get comfortable. She wasn't a seasoned rider. "How long do you think we have to go?" she asked the mare.

Jewel snorted and continued to move forward. She ducked under a large spiderweb. Shine was not paying attention, and the sticky strands caught her full in the face.

"Yuck! Ugh!" She peeled the web from her face. "Watch out, Jewel," she said. "Couldn't you give me some kind of warning?"

Jewel stopped and turned to look at Shine.

Shine met her eyes and felt sudden shame. "I'm sorry," she said. "I'm the one who should be paying attention."

After wandering for a time, they came around a corner and stopped. Before them was a metal door with four enormous sapphires on it. Shine read aloud the words carved on a wooden sign that hung below the gems.

IF YOU WOULD PASS
THEN CHOOSE ARIGHT.
IF YOU PICK WRONG
PREPARE TO FIGHT.

"Choose what?" Shine slid from Jewel's back, stretched her legs, and then moved to stand at the mare's head.

Together, they gazed up at the jewels set in the door. They all looked different, even though they were all sapphires. "I guess we have to pick the right gem to be allowed through. Which do you think we should pick, Jewel?"

Jewel pawed the ground with her forehoof as if to say, *I don't have a clue!*

Shine's heart sank. "I guess it's up to me," she said. "Mother used to repair Mrs. Marshall's jewelry. She showed me how to look for flaws. Maybe I can remember what she taught me." She bit her lip. "But I wonder what happens if I choose wrong?"

Jewel just blew out her breath in a gust.

"Only one way to find out," Shine murmured. She breathed deep, and then lifted her head and faced the gems.

Three had less shine and one of those had a hairline flaw. Only one looked perfect.

"I think it's the second from the

left," Shine said. She crossed her fingers, and then reached out and pressed the sapphire.

It sank into a socket. With a terrific groan, the door slid open. Shine let out a breath of relief.

Beyond the doorway, there was complete darkness. Before Shine could reach for her lantern, a light appeared. It came from Jewel—the gems in her forehead were shining, lighting the way. Shine smiled and laid her head on the mare's neck. "You are amazing!"

The *clip-clop* of Jewel's sure hooves filled the silence as they traveled through a new labyrinth of stone tunnels. They traveled up, and then down, and then up again, always turning left.

The light from Jewel's gems swung with the movement of the mare's head. Beyond the circle of the gems' glow was utter blackness. It seemed like night to Shine, but she had no way to know. She lost all sense of time passing. Had they been in these tunnels for an hour? A day? A week? Her eyelids began to droop. She forced them open.

Again and again they came to a place where the tunnel forked. Again and again Jewel turned left. But then, at one intersection, she balked.

"The map said to go left," Shine pointed out. She was so tired. She wanted to find the vault and be done with it.

Jewel skittered sideways, nickering uneasily.

"If we go the wrong way, we might never get out of here," Shine argued. "The map said left, Jewel. I think we should stick to it."

Jewel snorted. After a moment she moved reluctantly into the left tunnel.

As they traveled ever deeper into the ground, the tunnel floor grew rough. The path was littered with lumps of rock and shards of enormous colored crystals. Shine could hear stones falling behind them from time to time. Jewel still seemed hesitant.

"What is it? What's wrong?" Shine asked. Her voice shook. Jewel's nervousness was catching.

Another stone fell in the tunnel behind them, hitting the ground with a *thwock*. Jewel spooked, jumping sideways. She turned her head to look behind them. Shine turned, too.

The stones and gem shards behind them were swelling and moving! Before Shine's eyes, a handful of pebbles clattered toward each other, forming themselves into a rough head and torso. Long, sharp crystals skittered across the floor and attached themselves to the torso. The rock creature stood up jerkily. Jewel danced in fear and Shine shuddered.

Shine's eyes had adjusted to the dark, and now she could see beyond the circle of dim light cast by Jewel's gems. The tunnel was swarming with rock creatures! Their green eyes glowed. Their arms and legs were like shards of broken glass, razor sharp on the ends.

"Jewel!" Shine gasped.

With a ringing neigh, Jewel took off down the tunnel. Shine held tight as the mare leaped into a gallop, away from the creatures. Her hooves spewed dust and gem shards into the air. The tunnel twisted and turned. Shine wasn't even sure if they were going the right way anymore. All she could do was hang on. But then Jewel stopped so suddenly that Shine almost tumbled over the mare's neck. She peered ahead and almost screamed.

Their way forward was blocked by dozens more rock creatures. They were surrounded.

Jewel pranced and danced. The creatures crept toward the mare and the girl. A chopping sound echoed off the tunnel walls. With horror, Shine realized that it came from the creatures gnashing their jagged crystal teeth. One snapped at Jewel's front hoof, and Shine saw blood trickle down.

Jewel reared. Shine let out a yelp as a rock creature formed from the low ceiling of the tunnel. As it reached for her with sharp crystal fingers, she twisted away. "Leave us alone!" she cried. "Stop it!"

Jewel swung her head from side to side, snapping at the creatures that were trying to swarm up her flanks. That's when Shine noticed: Whenever the light from Jewel's forehead gems hit one of the creatures, it would jump away and cover its head.

"Light! They're afraid of light!" Shine yelled. Her fingers scrabbled at her pocket, where she'd stashed the glowfood. Could she get the lantern going, to add more light?

She scooped up all the pellets her fingers found. Jewel was moving so much that she didn't dare let go of the mare's mane. Somehow, one-handed, she managed to open the lantern panel and toss the food to the glowworms.

As they began to eat, the lantern began to glow, brighter and brighter. Shine held it high over her head. The ring of light around her and Jewel grew wider, and the rock creatures fell back.

By the light of the lantern, Shine spotted a narrow tunnel opening that led off to the left. "That way," she called, pointing. Jewel sped toward it.

The new tunnel was even narrower than the one they'd just left. Shine could practically touch the walls with her outstretched fingers. She had to lean forward like a jockey to keep her head from hitting the ceiling as Jewel galloped.

But at the far end, both girl and mare could see a faint glow. Somewhere ahead of them was light—and light meant safety from the rock creatures. Shine could hear them, clattering along in the shadows behind Jewel.

Jewel stretched her neck out, pounding toward the distant glow. Sweat rose and became foam on her neck.

Shine clung tight, her hands buried in the mare's mane. They wheeled around a corner and spun onward, galloping toward the light.

he light grew stronger and brighter. And with it, the rock creatures fell farther and farther behind.

Finally, Shine could no longer see or hear them. She lowered the lantern and reattached it to her belt. Jewel dropped her pace from a gallop to a canter, and finally to a trot. She snorted and heaved, her head hung low, spent from the long run.

"You outran them, Jewel," Shine told her. She shuddered. "Ugh! What were those things? I've never seen anything like them in my life!"

Jewel was breathing more evenly now. Shine rubbed the mare's neck gently. "You really were amazing," she said.

They turned another corner, and Shine saw the source of the light. It came from inside a cavernous opening in the left wall of the tunnel. "I guess that's a left turn," Shine said.

They stepped through. Shine stared in wonder at the walls of the cavern. The rocks and ledges were encrusted with sharp crystals. They grew outward in spikes. White light glowed within each one of them. They shimmered on the walls like gigantic diamonds.

"Wow!" Shine said, gaping. "I wonder if I could break some of them off and take them? They are so beautiful."

Jewel shook her head hard.

"All right," Shine assured her. "I'll leave them alone."

Jewel still seemed antsy. She kept sidestepping and twitching her coat as if to shrug off imaginary flies. Shine couldn't understand it. *She* was thrilled to be away from the rock creatures and in this beautiful, bright cavern.

Jewel picked up her pace, trotting though the middle of the cavern. Shine gazed around her at the walls, entranced by the sparkling crystals. But when she turned to glance behind, she frowned in puzzlement.

The entrance to the cavern wasn't there anymore.

Was she looking in the wrong place? Shine peered from side to side. But there was no sign of the opening, even though it had been quite large.

Also, the room looked a lot smaller than it had when they entered. . . .

That's when she realized it. The crystals were growing, filling in the empty space. Growing fast!

Shine gasped. "The crystals are alive!" Fear brimmed in her voice. First the rock creatures, now this! Why was

this happening? Why were the rocks and cave walls out to get them?

Jewel broke into a gallop once more, crossing to the opposite side of the cavern and bursting out into a tunnel there. The crystals expanded like wildfire, shooting down the tunnel behind them.

"We're going to be skewered!" Shine yelled. She leaned over Jewel's shoulders, holding tight. She gripped with her knees until her legs ached.

Jewel careened around a curve. Shine pushed Gertrude deep down into her jacket pocket with one hand. The wind whipped through her hair, burned tears from her eyes, and took her breath away. Jewel shot around another bend. Her hooves scrabbled on the stone floor and she stumbled. It took everything Shine had to keep her seat. She knew Jewel was doing her best to keep ahead of the surging crystal. All she could to do was hang on.

They were on a straight part now, and in front of them the tunnel seemed to stretch on for miles. Jewel had drawn ahead of the crystals—for now. But Shine knew the mare could not keep up this pace forever, especially on top of the run she'd just had. And when she slowed, the crystals would catch up.

A hard knot settled in Shine's stomach. What were they going to do?

Jewel galloped on. Shine winced as she heard the mare's labored breathing. Then Jewel's ears pricked forward.

Peering into the dimness ahead, Shine saw a small, oddly shaped building to the right of the track. What was it doing here, so far underground in the deserted tunnels? Shine wondered. "Maybe we'll find help there!" she yelled to Jewel. Jewel hurtled toward it at a full gallop, and then pulled to a shuddering stop in front of it.

Jewel panted. Lather had crept from her neck to her sides, wetting

Shine's calves. Shine slid off; Jewel didn't need to be carrying her weight right now. They circled the building.

The back part had been carved from a hollowed-out section of boulder that stuck out into the tunnel. The front was made of piled stones held together with crumbling mortar.

Would it protect them? Could the diamond crystals pierce through stone?

Shine laid her hand on Jewel's side. "Can you fit inside? The doorway looks so small." She began to sob. "What are we going to do?"

The picture of a brass bell formed in her mind, a vision sent by Jewel. She jerked up her head. "A bell? What are you trying to tell me?"

Shine pulled open the sagging door and stepped in. On three sides, shelves and cupboards had been cunningly carved right into the stone walls. A stone workbench stood against the fourth wall. All sorts of jeweler's tools hung from hooks above it, although a few of the hooks were empty. She stood still for a moment, marveling at the treasure trove of tools.

A leather-bound book lay on a workbench. Shine flipped it open. It was a master jeweler's manual.

From the doorway Jewel neighed urgently. Shine put the book down—no time to study it now! She moved to the shelves. Rows of wooden drawers hung from their undersides. Shine slid a drawer open—and blinked at the bars of silver and gold that lay inside. Any other time she would have been fascinated, but right now the only emotion she could feel was terror.

She opened another drawer, and another, increasingly frantic. Some were empty. Many held gold, copper, and silver jeweler's wire, or crystal beads in glass containers. But Shine saw nothing that seemed like it might make a good weapon for fighting giant expanding crystals.

Outside the cabin the mare snorted and pawed, tearing up the gravel path. Shine ran to the doorway and stared down the dusty tunnel. Her heart banged against her ribs as she saw that the crystals were in sight.

Only one cupboard remained unsearched. Shine threw open the doors. Her eyes widened. Inside, the shelves were lined with bells—dingy, tarnished bells of every shape and size. This was what Jewel wanted! Shine just didn't know why. . . .

She swept her hand over the shelf, pushing a line of small bells into her dress pocket. Then she grabbed two of the largest bells and ran outside. "Here," she said breathlessly, offering the big bells to Jewel. "Is this what you need?"

Jewel grasped one between her teeth and began to shake her head up and down, up and down. *Clang! Clang! Clang!* The bell's deep voice echoed down the tunnel.

Along with the pealing of the bell came a beautiful sound—the sound of crystal shattering and exploding. The bell's tone was destroying them!

Shine's mouth fell open in astonishment. Raising the other big bell high overhead, she began to ring it wildly. There was a huge groan and more cracking. The larger crystals began to shatter.

Shine had an idea. Still clanging away, she ran back inside the hut and grabbed a roll of silver wire from one of the drawers. She used pliers to clip off a length, and then strung the smaller bells on it as fast as she could, making a bell necklace to place around Jewel's neck.

She darted back out and draped the necklace over Jewel's withers. Jewel rubbed her head along Shine's arm encouragingly, and the girl climbed aboard. Jewel shot down the path like a racehorse out of the starting gate. As she ran, the bells around her neck tinkled.

Shine hung on with one hand.

She held the largest bell high in the air and rang it for all she was worth. They bolted down the passageway, listening to the crash and tinkle of crystals shattering behind them.

Jewel exploded around a curve, moving uphill. Then she slammed to a stop, shooting Shine up on her neck. Shine regained her balance and peered ahead. Before them, completely blocking the tunnel, was the largest crystal of all. It was bigger even than Jewel herself. As they watched, it began to expand.

Shine tamped down panic. There was no time for it. Raising her arms over her head, she began to ring the big bell again. Her arms ached and sweat ran down her cheeks, making strands of hair stick to her face and arms.

Still, the crystal pushed menacingly toward them, powerful and growing. The bell wasn't working!

And there was nowhere left to run.

8

Jewel shook her head hard and rose on her hind legs. The crystal was huge, shining, reflecting in her face.

Shine closed her eyes and hung onto Jewel's mane, waiting for the crystal to crush them. Suddenly, she felt herself spinning. She opened her eyes.

Jewel had whirled around, kicked out with her hind legs and nailed the gem with both back hooves. An explosion filled the air as the crystal shattered into a million sparkling pieces. They showered down around Jewel and Shine like silver rain.

Ahead of them, the tunnel was clear.

Shine slid from Jewel's back, buried her face in a soft brown shoulder, and began to weep. "Oh, Jewel," she sobbed. "I've never been so scared in all my life."

Warmth emanated from within Jewel, tender and comforting. It flowed into Shine's hands and down her arms, building as it spread. It filled her with strength.

"Thank you," Shine whispered to the mare. "I can't imagine doing this without you."

She stood for a moment longer as her sobs turned to sniffles and her body stopped shaking. As the terror passed, her brain began to work again.

"Rock creatures, crystal creatures—I've never heard of anything like that in the stories my parents told me. Why did they attack us?" she wondered aloud. "Do you think someone sent them? Do you think they were trying to keep us from finding the Rolanddotter vault?"

Jewel snorted, huffing breath through her nose. To Shine, it was as if the mare had said aloud, *Let them try!*

She grinned. "Yes, let them. We can do anything if we stick together!"

Shine swung herself onto Jewel's back once again and they moved on.

We will find the vault, Shine thought. *We will.*

They rode for some time. Shine was amazed at how varied the underground world of Stonelory was. Some of the tunnels were dark and rough-hewn. Others were like broad avenues, walls lined with smooth gray stone. Once they came upon a vast cavern completely filled with glowworms, all busily munching on moss. Their combined glow was so bright, Shine had to shade her eyes as they passed through.

At another point they passed through a cavern where a rockfall had left a wide gap open to the sky. Shine was startled to see it was full daylight outside. Sun poured into the cavern, which was overgrown with lush green plants and huge flowers. A waterfall cascaded through the middle, and birds darted and sang in the leaves. It was like a tropical grotto.

Then, abruptly, the path made a sharp turn and dipped back underground. As darkness folded around them once more, Shine felt her spirits plunge. "I wish we could have stayed in the light," she murmured. Jewel nodded her head in agreement, but plodded on.

A while later, Shine gradually became aware of a distant, muffled thumping up ahead. It grew louder as they moved onward. "It sounds like someone is banging a drum," she commented.

The drumbeats were slow and rhythmic. After a while, the steady beat made Shine sleepy. Her head bobbed with each of Jewel's strides, and she had to force her eyelids open when the mare stepped into a cavernous room and halted.

As she took in the scene, though, her eyes grew wide and her exhaustion fled. She slid off Jewel's back and took a step forward, staring.

Creamy white marble floors stretched in front of them. Tall white columns stood in a circle around the edges of the room. It reminded Shine of the throne room in one of Grandmother's fairy tales.

And everywhere she looked, there were life-sized dolls—slumped in chairs, on the floor, on marble benches. They drooped against tables and leaned on the columns. In the center of the room, on a raised platform sat a king doll and a queen doll, placed perfectly on grand gold-and-purple thrones. Royal soldier dolls leaned on each other nearby.

Shine couldn't believe what she was seeing. It must be the most elaborate dollhouse in the world! But whose was it?

She looked at Jewel to see her reaction. The horse stood still, also taking in the room.

In the corner, a band of dolls were dressed as musicians with instruments. In their midst was the only creature moving in the throne room—a lone drummer doll, beating a slow, repetitive rhythm on his drum.

The dull sound made Shine tired and sad. Taking another step forward, she sank down on the cold marble floor and clasped her arms around her knees. She was so sleepy . . . if only she could rest for a few minutes. . . .

She lay down on her side, curled up on the chilly stone. A little nap, that was all she needed. Just a nap.

No, a faint voice inside her said. *Something is not right.*

"I'll figure it out after my nap," Shine murmured. Her tongue felt oddly thick.

She let her eyes close. Or rather, she *tried* to let her eyes close. But they seemed to be stuck open.

Alarmed, Shine reached up to feel her eyelids.

Her arms wouldn't move! Her fingers were frozen in place!

What's happening? she tried to shout. But her jaw was locked shut.

I'm turning into a doll! she realized. Horror filled her, but there was nothing she could do. None of her muscles would obey the commands her brain was screaming at them.

Jewel, help me!

Jewel spun around as if she'd heard the words Shine could not speak. She let out a sharp whinny and raced across the room until she was standing in front of the drummer doll.

Shine couldn't turn her head, but out of the corner of her eye she saw that Jewel had begun to execute the fanciest of dressage moves. It looked like a sort of dance. She tapped her hooves on the cool stone floor in a complex rhythm. She pranced faster and faster.

The doll drummer responded, drumming faster and faster.

As the rhythm sped up, Shine felt warmth spreading down her limbs again, life returning. As soon as she could stand, she ran to join Jewel in the dance. Side by side with the mare, she tapped her feet and swung her arms madly. The drummer picked up his pace even more.

Around the room, the other doll musicians began to move, to blink and stand straight. One by one they joined in on their own instruments—a clarinet, a horn, a flute, a violin. The sound was a celebration of life.

Shine leaned close to Jewel.

"Living dolls!" she whispered. "They must have been under some kind of spell. Keep dancing, Jewel. Let's bring them all back to life!"

The thrill of movement brought out supreme beauty in Jewel, just as it had in the dressage ring. The gems on her brow sparkled, a pulsing, joyful light show.

Shine tapped her feet in time with Jewel's dancing hooves and looked from face to face. All around the room, the dolls were coming alive. They marched and swung their arms stiffly in time with the music.

Shine's gaze stopped on one of the dolls that had been lying on the floor. Clad in a stiff brocade gown, it had long, dark hair with flecks of silver-gray in it. As it rose, Shine saw that its movements were fluid, not stiff like those of the other dolls.

As the doll turned to face her, Shine let out a cry of joy.

"Mother!"

9

*S*hine bolted forward and fell into her mother's arms. "I missed you so much!" she cried. She raised her head to gaze into her mother's deep brown eyes, to stare at the beloved face she'd pictured in her mind every single day since she'd gone.

Tears stood in Mother's eyes as she stroked her daughter's hair. "I missed you, too," she replied. Shine was flooded with happiness. Even if they didn't find the Rolanddotter vault, at least they had found each other.

"What happened?" she babbled, her words tumbling over one another. "Where have you been? How did you find your way here? How long have you been a doll?"

Instead of answering, Mother's gaze moved to a spot over Shine's shoulder. Alarm filled her face.

Shine spun around to see the doll king leap from his throne, his heavy purple robes swaying. "Halt!" he yelled.

His voice echoed across the room. The musicians fell silent as he stalked across to stand in front of Shine and her mother. Behind her, Shine sensed that Jewel had stopped dancing. The mare stepped delicately forward until she was next to Shine. Mother gave Jewel a single, startled look.

The king glared at them. His crown was tilted to one side. "I am the chief guardian of the Rolanddotter vault, and that thief is mine," he said, pointing at Shine's mother. His speech was jerky and mechanical. "You cannot free her. This is her jail, her punishment for trying to rob the vault."

Shine's heart skipped a beat. They wanted to keep Mother as their prisoner?

Then she thought, *Guardian of the Rolanddotter vault? That means it must be near!*

Behind the king, the queen pushed herself up rigidly, unbending at the waist as she rose from her throne. She came to stand beside the king. Stiff petticoats held her lacy dress in a dome around her, and layers of lace fell from her waist to the floor. Red yarn hair was piled high under her silver crown. Her face was smooth porcelain, with rosy cheeks and lips and wide, sparkling blue eyes. They were made of sapphires, Shine realized, looking at them more closely. And the king's were emeralds.

Six soldier dolls followed the queen, forming a line and snapping to attention.

Shine's mind whirled. Although they were just dolls, she had no doubt that they could be dangerous. The air almost crackled with tension. How was she going to get Mother free and also find and open the Rolanddotter vault?

Gertrude! she thought. *Gertrude is the key to the vault. And I have her. Maybe I can strike a bargain!*

Shine reached into her jacket and pulled out her beloved doll. She held Gertrude high. "This is the key to the Rolanddotter vault," she said, her voice quivering. "We have the key—and therefore we have the right to open the vault. *And* to leave in peace."

The effect was immediate, but not what Shine had intended. The throne room erupted with shouts.

"The princess! The lost one!"

"They stole her!"

"Our poor princess—just look at her!"

Raising her hands for silence, the

queen spoke. Her pleasant, painted face could not display any emotion, but rage quivered in her voice. "That is my daughter," she declared. "What have you done to her?"

Shine's head was spinning. *Gertrude? Their daughter? Gertrude is a doll princess?*

The king shook his scepter at Shine. "Where are her eyes? What happened to her face? You have killed her, you monsters!"

Shine gripped Gertrude tighter. "I—I didn't. I couldn't! She's my doll! I love her. But she's very old."

"She is a royal princess! She was stolen from us!" The king stepped closer. Now he was only an arm's length away. Shine backed up, fear rushing in her veins. Jewel gave her a nudge with her nose.

The drummer doll began to beat his drum again—this time with a warlike roll. Dolls surged forward, surrounding

Shine and Jewel and Mother. There was a ringing sound as all the soldier dolls drew their swords as one. Their blank faces were somehow more terrifying than faces full of rage could ever be.

Shine sprang onto Jewel's back, yanking Mother on behind her. Jewel leaped clear over the king and queen and ran for all she was worth, galloping out of the doll room and down the tunnel from which they had come. Behind them the drum beat steadily. When Shine looked back, she saw columns of doll soldiers marching in pursuit. There were so many, more than she had realized when they were in the room.

Shine clung tight to Jewel. Mother clung to Shine's waist. Shine glanced down at Gertrude, whom she'd stuffed back into her jacket.

Should I have given Gertrude to the king? After all, she is his daughter. Families should not be separated.

But she is the key. And more than

that, she's mine—my best friend!

No, she isn't, a voice inside her retorted. *Look at her poor battered face, her missing eyes. Do friends treat friends that way?*

Jewel's forehead gems sent beams of white radiance outward, lighting the dark tunnel. Dust spewed from the path, and sweat rose on the mare's shoulders. Under the weight of two people, she was tiring more quickly.

They flashed past the grotto and the glowworm cave. Sooner than she would have thought possible, Shine saw the jeweler's cabin ahead. She felt Jewel's pace falter. The mare slowed to a walk and Shine listened. Behind them, faint but relentless, came the beat of the doll drummer. The dolls were still on their trail. And ahead were the deadly expanding crystals, and then the hideous rock creatures.

For the first time, Shine felt utterly helpless. *How will this end?* she wondered. *How can we possibly get out alive?*

$\mathcal{A}$t the cabin, Shine and Mother dismounted so that Jewel could rest and recover. Shine pulled Gertrude out of her jacket and gazed down at the battered old doll.

"Gertrude can come to life," she marveled. "She has the ability to walk and speak, just like those other dolls." She leaned closer to her beloved doll. "All these years you've listened to my problems . . . all that time, have you been able to understand me?"

The doll's eyeless face stared up at Shine.

Shine turned to Mother. "How did Gertrude come to be in our family? And what happened to her eyes?"

Mother gave a helpless shrug. "She was passed to me like that, and to Grandmother before me. But I loved her as she was, just the way you do."

Shine felt a terrible sadness. She touched the doll's face, smoothing down the soft red hair, fingering the lace-trimmed frock. Poor Gertrude, trapped in her frozen state. How could Shine not have realized what she really was?

A tear welled up and splashed onto the doll's battered face. Then another.

"I want to fix her eyes," Shine said. It was the only thing she could think to do. At least when the doll army arrived, they would see that Gertrude had proper eyes again.

"But how?" Mother asked.

Shine shrugged. "We're jewel crafters," she pointed out. "We should be able to figure it out."

Jewel shook her mane and neighed in agreement. Stepping forward, she lowered her head and Shine saw that two gems in her brow had come loose—a sapphire and an emerald.

She caught her breath. "You are offering your own gems? You think I should use them to make Gertrude's new eyes?"

Jewel neighed again, stamping a forehoof for emphasis.

Mother nodded enthusiastically. "Gems for eyes. Perfect!"

Shine gently took the gems out of their settings. Behind them, two new jewels were already growing to fill the spaces. Shine studied the gemstones in her palm. She shifted her gaze to Gertrude and back to the gems again. They would need to be cut to the right size and shape. . . .

"I've never cut gems, but I think

it's important that I do this myself," she said. "Mother, will you help?"

"Of course," Mother replied.

Shine hurried into the stone hut. The jeweler's manual was on the table, but there was no time to read it—the doll army would be there soon.

Mother stood at her shoulder to guide her.

Shine bent over the emerald first. Even though it was rough, she could tell the uncut stone was of the finest quality. It reflected intense dark green shot with lighter, almost glowing tones. She turned to the tools hanging on the wall and chose a delicate chisel with a diamond tip.

"Lay the tip near the center of the stone," Mother instructed. "Then tap it with the mallet. Gently—gently!"

Shine held her breath and tapped gently. Mother nodded her approval.

A flake of emerald fell away. Shine moved the diamond tip to the side and tapped again. Another piece fell away.

Carefully, she worked her way around the edge of the emerald, tapping away excess stone, revealing the flawless gem within. When she was finished, she had crafted a perfect oval eye for her beloved friend.

"Perfect!" Mother declared.

Next, Shine turned to the sapphire. The glassy blue crystal reflected tones of dark blue and purple. She knew her goal would be to bring out the blue and make the cut match the shape of the oval emerald eye. Carefully, she set to work.

Cutting the sapphire seemed easier than the emerald had been—perhaps because Shine was gaining confidence. Soon she had a perfectly cut oval, glowing blue, an ideal match for the emerald.

When at last Shine lifted her head, she heard the sounds her intense concentration had blocked out. The drumbeats were close now! She stepped outside to stand beside Jewel. The gems she had cut were cupped in her hand. "I'm ready," she told Jewel and Mother.

Mother pulled her close. "I am so proud of you," she whispered. "No matter what happens, remember that."

Jewel nickered softly, blowing on Shine's cheek with her sweet-smelling breath.

Shine drew Gertrude from inside her jacket. She saw the splashes of her own tears still damp on the doll's soft face. She set the emerald on the spot where an eye should go.

The gem seemed to glow for a moment as though a light had switched on inside it. It settled into Gertrude's empty socket.

Shine blinked. The cheek below the emerald eye had grown visibly rounder and rosier.

Jewel pawed the ground. The soldiers were just around the bend. *Bum, bum, barum-bum-bum,* the drumbeats rang out.

Shine placed the sapphire where

Gertrude's other eye should go. She lined it up it carefully with the emerald eye and watched in awe as the jewel settled into place. Gertrude's other cheek grew plump and rosy.

And then she blinked.

Shine held her breath as Gertrude's whole face flushed with rosy color. Her new eyes began to move and sparkle—one blue, one green.

"Hello, Shine!" said Gertrude.

"Hello, Gertrude!" Shine said automatically. This was so strange!

"I always wondered what color your hair was," the doll said in a conversational tone. "It's very pretty. Like roasted chestnuts." She blinked again. "Thank you for my new eyes. They feel just *wonderful*! Much better than the old ones."

Shine began to giggle. She couldn't help it. Right before her very eyes, her doll had come to life!

Then she realized Gertrude was

also growing. Already she was twice her usual size. Shine set the doll carefully on the tunnel floor. Within minutes Gertrude was the same height as Shine herself.

Jewel neighed urgently, and Shine snapped back to the present. Looking up, she saw with alarm that the first line of soldiers was coming around a curve in the tunnel. They marched in perfect unison, their swords held out before them.

"I'm glad to have given you your eyes, but I'm afraid we don't have much time together. Those dolls think we kidnapped and tortured you. They're going to kill us!" Shine told Gertrude. Her voice shook.

Gertrude's painted face didn't change, of course, but somehow Shine could feel the doll grow solemn. "No harm will come to you," Gertrude said. "Those are my people. And my father will listen to me."

By now the soldier dolls stood in a

circle around Shine, Jewel, and Mother. The king spoke up. "You will pay the price for what you have done to our daughter," he said.

Gertrude stepped out from behind Shine. "Father! Mother!"

"Gertrude?" The king rushed forward, and then stopped short, looking Gertrude up and down as if doubting she were real. Behind him, the queen clasped her hands together. "Are you all right?"

"Of course I am. Oh, Father, Mother!" Gertrude hurried forward, holding out her arms. The king and queen rushed to embrace her. Shine thought she saw a sparkle of wetness in the king's doll eyes as he hugged his daughter.

After a moment, though, he withdrew. "They must still be punished for hurting you."

"No, Father!" Gertrude's voice rang out. She stood between the king and queen, a hand in each of theirs. "It's true,

I was frozen for a long time." She glanced over at Jewel and Shine and Mother. "But you're wrong about Shine and her mother. They would never hurt me. They have always loved and cared for me.

"When Sigga and Sara chose me as the key, I never told you, because I feared the knowledge might put you in danger. Instead, I asked Jewel to take me away from the vault and hide me. Sara found a spell to make me small so that I wouldn't attract attention. And Jewel found me a home with Shine's great-grandmother's great-grandmother."

Shine glanced at her mother. Mother's eyes were wide with wonder as Gertrude continued her tale.

"The one who took my eyes was a treasure seeker. He stole me from Shine's family and removed my eyes to keep me powerless. But Jewel rescued me from him and took me back to the Anders family. They took care of me, and now Shine has given me eyes again."

The king rotated to gaze at Shine. The soldiers stood in straight lines, waiting for the king's next order. He waved at them to be at ease, and then stepped forward, standing before Shine and her mother.

"I see you now for who you are," he said, "and I thank you for the love you gave my daughter all these many years."

Mother stepped forward. "I did not come to rob the Rolanddotter vault," she declared. "My ancestors were the Rolandsgaard Castle jewel crafters, but we have fallen on hard times. I thought that if I could retrieve our old crafting tools, I might be able to use them to revive our ancient art." Her mouth quirked in a smile. "It was only after I found the tools that I came to your throne room. I simply wanted to see the place I'd heard about all my life."

Shine listened in astonishment. *What?* She had thought Mother *was* planning to take some of the treasure!

But as she mulled over Mother's words, she realized something. Having their position back was even more important than riches. A craft, a profession would bring a satisfaction that riches alone could not achieve. Even if she weren't wealthy, if Shine were a respected jewel crafter, people like Jeremiah Marshall could never make her feel worthless again.

The king glanced at the queen, and she nodded. Then he spoke again. "The guardians of the Rolanddotter vault must never forget the castle jewel crafters." He turned. "Come. I will lead you to the vault."

The king and queen led the way back to the throne room, one walking on either side of their long-lost daughter. Jewel pranced down the trail beside Shine and Mother, her forehead sparkling. Shine reached out to touch the mare's flank.

Back at the throne room, Gertrude

turned to Shine. "No flesh-and-blood creature may enter the Rolanddotter vault," she said. "Only I can enter. But you have earned the right to see."

Shine followed Gertrude past overturned chairs and marble benches to the back of the hall. The king escorted them up a set of steps. At the top he pushed a carved ivory button. A paneled wall slid open. Behind it was a thick bronze door without a knob or handle of any kind.

Gertrude stepped forward. "Lady, I request access to the Rolanddotter treasure."

Shine stared in amazement as an image took shape, the form of a tall lady wearing a long, elegant dress of pale blue. Purple orchids were entwined in her thick blond braids. The ghostly figure was Sigga Rolanddotter! Wait until she told Jack about this!

"May I see the Rolanddotter treasure?" Gertrude asked.

"You may, Gertrude," Sigga replied.

In the blink of an eye, Sigga was adorned with jewels. A spangled tiara kissed her brow. Her arms jingled with jeweled bracelets, rings, and necklaces, and at her side was a long, silver-hilted sword resting inside a gem-encrusted, leather-bound sheath. Shine stepped back, awestruck by the splendor of the Valkyrie.

Sigga's gaze softened as she caught sight of Jewel. "Jewel, my friend!" she exclaimed.

Shine turned to look at Jewel, and her eyes widened even more. Jewel was now adorned in a sparkling bridle and saddle, a silk blanket, and a crown of her own, the jewels matching those that Sigga wore. Twelve multicolored gems spun around Jewel in a luminous orbit.

Behind Sigga, jeweled goblets, golden plates, and other precious objects lay heaped. Shine's eyes stopped on a fantastic statue of a bay mare, carved out of a single piece of some deep reddish stone. Only six inches high, it was a perfect likeness of Jewel, right down to the gems in the forehead. It was beautiful!

Gertrude spoke to Sigga. "Shine and her mother are descended from the jewel crafters of Rolandsgaard Castle. May each take an item of their choosing?"

Sigga nodded. "They may."

Shine's heart leaped.

"Thank you, but I respectfully decline," Mother said softly. "The riches of the vault must be preserved for the return of a Rolanddotter to North of North. I came only for my crafting tools. I need nothing more."

At first Shine thought, *That's crazy!* She wasn't going to turn down a gift from the Rolanddotter vault. She'd come a long way to get it!

But then, as she gazed from treasure to treasure, she realized that those things did not seem so important anymore. Her heart was full with the friends and family, new and old, she had found on this journey. Her mother, Jewel, Gertrude—how could she want for anything else?

Shine turned to Gertrude. She took the doll's hand in her own.

"I choose you," she said. With her other hand she reached out and stroked Jewel's mane. "And you, Jewel. Your friendship is what matters most to me."

Jewel snorted softly and nuzzled Shine's hand. Gertrude smiled. "I'll be your friend, now and always. And Jewel will bring me back to you, but not today. Today I will spend with my family and my people."

Sigga smiled approvingly. "Wise choices, both of you." She looked at Shine. "Now go," she added. "Your passage home will be a safe one."

Then she was gone. The royal treasure faded, too, and then vanished.

Mother put her hand on Shine's shoulder. She leaned down and kissed her daughter's hair.

Shine sighed, exhausted but at peace. She'd found Mother. She'd found a lifelong friend in Jewel. She'd restored Gertrude to life and to her family, and now she knew the Rolanddotter vault was safe. She knew, too, that there were things in this world more important than gold and jewels.

Jewel lifted her head high in the air and whinnied. Shine threw her head back and laughed out loud. The echo of her laughter joined Jewel's joyous whinny.

"Come," Mother said with a smile. "Let's go home."

t dawn the following morning, Marta woke with a start. She wasn't sure if she was dreaming or if she had just heard a horse whinny. She tiptoed to the window, careful not to wake her mother or brother. She gasped when she saw a winged horse standing outside. With the intricate gem-studded pattern on her forehead and gossamerlike mane and tail, Marta knew immediately who the majestic creature was.

It was Nike!

Marta rubbed her eyes. *I must*

be dreaming, she thought. She quickly wrapped her quilt around her shoulders and walked out the door. She was standing just footsteps away from the beautiful horse. The dry grass felt scratchy under her bare feet. *If I were dreaming, then I wouldn't be able to feel this itchy grass.* A rush of excitement flooded through her. *Could Nike really be outside my very own house?*

Marta took in the horse's magnificent wings and glowing eyes. She took a step closer to the horse and felt her whole body tingle as if a magnetic force were pulling her forward. She wanted to run right up to Nike, but she sensed it was not the proper thing to do. Instead, she bowed her head slightly. In response, Nike bowed.

Raising her eyes, Marta gazed at the large, chestnut brown horse, taking in all her splendor. The horse began to preen and clean her wings. Marta was in awe. "Your beauty, your grace," she said to Nike, "you are the most magnificent horse I've ever seen. Are you really . . . Nike?"

The horse stood proudly, emanating a soft glow.

Marta couldn't believe it. Nike! The real Nike that she had dreamed about every day for as long as she could remember was right here in front of her own house!

"This is the most wonderful thing that has ever happened to me!" Marta gasped. She ran inside to wake her parents and tell them the amazing news.

Go to
www.bellasara.com
and enter the webcode below.
Enjoy!

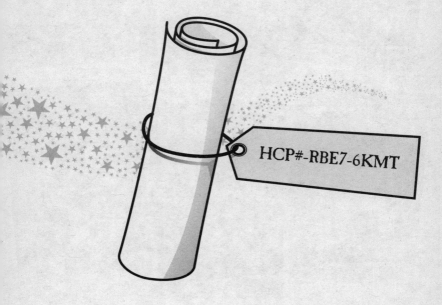

HCP#-RBE7-6KMT